1

This is a work of fiction, Names, characters, places, and incidents either are the product of the author's imagination or are used fictitiously. Any resemblance to actual persons, living or dead. Events, or locales is entirely coincidental.

By Masaka None

Copyright 2022 Masaka None

2 TABLE OF CONTENTS

3 FOREWORD

What is more unpredictable than life? The universe decides to turn around toby's life by taking what mattered the mist to him, someone he would cry to when in pain, his mom. Just when we thought that's the worst that could happen, Jackson is deprived off Toby, with the whole family turning against him, he is left lonely, all alone facing, and in war with the white walls of his humungous inn. Its amazing how one event can alter a sequence of events following it. From a 'HAPPY FAMILY' to working towards being a 'happy family again.' The death of Gladys led to war and unsettledness within the family. Things end up escalating, bloodshed everywhere, trusts broken, and marriages broken. The book explores the story of how one event altered all that came after

4 ABOUT THE AUTHOR

MASAKA JOHANNES NONE was born in Olverton, Northwest, South Africa, on June 17,2002. During the brainstorming and writing of this book he was studying toward an accounting science degree at the university of the Witwatersrand, South Africa. His work could be found across many, if not all online digital stores. He fell in love with writing at an early age of 11years old and has since then transformed into a lover of wordplay. He never looked back after publishing his first book *"THE LAST ONE OF MY KIND, CHOSEN TO DIE"*

CHAPTER 1: THE CORE TAKETH

He, just like all the other kids had dreams, saw the world as a little tiny thing where everything was possible, where every man's desire was attainable. Though bringest to him a rare thought -life can humble oneself. Toby lived with both his parents and believe me you; life was all about fun and his papas' purse was so fat even a 450pound heavyweight bodybuilder would not be able to carry. He was the brightest of his schoolmates and just like every other genius out there, he never thought someday the tables would turn.

He got whatever he wanted whenever he wanted. His mom, Gladys, was so loving and caring that you would wish she were thine. His father-that was his role-model, his living icon. It was one Friday when little toby carried the weight, he felt burdening his shoulders going home from school, only to find out that the string that held the family together; the core that the family fell to when in pain was gone.

 His eyes rolled round and round as he wondered how life would suddenly be without his mom. He ran to his room and cried till he could not feel the tears flowing down his cheeks no more. He was in such pain that he could barely move his hands to wipe off the tears. He remembered how naturing she was, how she always found ways to make him feel better and suddenly thought of how she would have comforted him if she were there. That is life -full of plethora of unforeseen occurrences, twists and turns, lessons, and corrections. Only had they known that it was the beginning of a foundering ship. Poor little Toby eye-witnessing the fall of the Smith empire.

 The burial of his mother was scheduled to be on the next Saturday. Families came in their own diverse ways; thou would be perplexed of how people unite only when a tragedy has bestowed. Funeral plans were already in motion but to toby it was as if everyone was celebrating except for him and his father. The smiles he saw on their faces and the laughter they all shared as they prepared for the burial was too puzzling and he so went back to his room.

The funeral day came; the day little Toby had to finally let go of all the happy memories they spent together, the vacations they had and the laughter they shared. Immediately after they were done, they all went back to the smith's inn where they enjoyed the after tears .it was not too late when Ahmir- Gladys's brother started the great debate. He insisted that Jackson (Toby's father) should marry one of Gladys's little sisters so that Toby would grow up with guidance from a female person. Although his father was always there during his times of need, the family vowed to confiscate toby from him if he did not marry Marry-Gladys's little sister. Jackson looked straight to where his biological relatives were sitting. He unblinkingly looked into their eyes one at a time as though someone who would dance with thy support, but only harsh he wouldst earn. For he was too fond of his late wife he had never imagined been affectionate towards someone again. Educated was he and vowed to convey thy topic to claws of law.

Meanwhile Toby could not resist the egregious topic and began releasing thy innocent water down his palpitating cheeks. His greatest wish was to help his father speak out, but he thought he would forfeit the battle as his father was already getting sniped out.

The whole family had the same reply to Jackson's words of involving the law. They all vowed to contest him by testifying against him. "If you think we are fools to let you lead this boy astray by spoiling him then you got another thing coming!"-said Ahmir

The house began to get even more peaceless and everyone suddenly had some to say against Jackson. Some even went far as saying Jackson was too incompetent to raise a kid alone as he had no male guardian while growing up. All those words started to feel like an unending song to his ears till he could not bear it anymore. He had tried to hold it for much longer to a point where he roared so loud the roof trembled and the inn went silent. Toby stood from his little spot. his clothes all wet as if he had just got out of the pool. the tears were still flowing endlessly down his cheeks when he said in his squeaky little voice- "I can't take this anymore, I wish mom was here to see how the world is without her," he paused to breathe "she would be so disappointed in all of you. You claim to be family, yet you want to separate me from my father. It's clear that the family has lost its core."

Jackson finally felt a moment of relief as the whole room went silent to listen to wise words from the small one. Just as he thought all was at peace the house started again. He realised that even if he bringeth law to solve thy matter it would all be a waste of time and resources besides Toby was too young and so by law had no capacity to reason, judge nor conclude. He did not want to let go of his only child but then he also did not want to marry Mary. He took Toby to his room to discuss the matter and how he felt about it. Toby did not want him to marry Mary and concluded that it would be best for him to go live with Ahmir and his wife, Sarah.

They went to the main room and told them thy conclusion verdict. "I shall channelise notes from my account to yours, Ahmir, every month" he further elaborated "you shall inform me if he needs something, as I cannot sleep elephantid when my son goes to divan hungry."

"Alright, stop with the bombastic words, there's no need to show off your fancy education" said Ahmir, mocking Jackson. They packed all his clothes into the suitcases his mom bought for their planned vacation. Soon Jackson was staring unto the white walls all alone in San Francisco. As for Toby, he was on his way to Louisiana with Ahmir and his wife.

CHAPTER 1: EYES OUT, IT GETS WORSE!!

Toby kept asking himself on the way why Ahmir insisted that he lived with them but still found himself wandering in a stuffed bush. They soon arrived at his new home in Louisiana. although the house was big, he felt like it was too insignificant compared to the palace he lived in back in San Francisco. He became used to living there as time went, he had already made a friend, Naomi. They became so close that they shared everything and talked about almost everything.

FEW YEARS LATER AFTER MOVING INTO LOUISIANA.........

Toby was turning 16 doing his senior year in high school. Throughout the previous years he established a reputation for himself. He was known for acing the academics some even went far as calling him "Apt"- apt meaning he was mentally quick. Naomi, well as for her she was more than a friend to him, they became the power couple of Louisiana High. It was at the beginning of his senior year when Ahmir and his wife called him into the living room one evening. "Son!" said Ahmir "the reason why we called you into this room is because we want to tell you that your father won't be giving you any allowance"

Toby was puzzled because he knew his father would never do that, but he suddenly questioned "is that why dad no longer visit us?" "Is it because he no longer wants anything to do with me?" he asked again. Ahmir replied by telling him that his father was a fool to desert him in such time and further assured him that he will be there for him. Toby thought what they told him was true and became destroyed in such a way that he couldn't sleep for two consecutive days.

Ahmir had planned this for the past years hence he insisted that Toby came to stay with them. All that he wanted was the Smiths inheritance. He knew that Toby was their only heir and consequently everything shall be passed down unto him. He wanted to make sure that Toby hated his father before he could carry out his mission of obliterating Jackson.

He googled pictures of Jackson with his female business associates and hired someone who can edit and photoshop images. The hired person did his job so well that even Ahmir believed in his own lies. One afternoon when Toby came back from school, he saw the picture and immediately had an emotional breakdown. For what he saw was traumatizing and couldn't believe how stupid he was to think his father wouldn't fall in love again. After seeing the pictures, he quickly ran to the mountains, to their (his and Naomi's) favourite spot.

"Did you see that?" Ahmir asked his wife

(They both laughed immediately after Toby ran out of the house)

For they had succeeded in their plan of destroying the Smiths empire and now all that was left was for Jackson to make a few calls and get done with Jackson meanwhile he was still receiving the monthly allowance the Jackson was sending Toby and the real reason why Jackson was no longer visiting is because of they told him they had moved to a new town, and he shall not step his foot in their new home. They had also greased their neighbour's (who works in the law industry) palms to draft a restraining order against Jackson.

MEANWHILE IN SAN FRANCISCO...

Jackson couldn't cope like he used to before. His businesses started to not do as well as they were doing before. Immediately after Ahmir showed him the restraining order, he realised that they were up to something and so transferred 95 percent of the money he had in his main account to his offshore account and only left a million in his main account. He then sold 8 of his cars and got left with a vintage Rolls Royce. He somehow foreseen that Ahmir and his wife were after his son's inheritance and the only way for them to get is for him to die.

He then hired someone to look after his home and car his Home. His name was Michael of whom was identical to him in terms of physical and facial appearance. One had to be so close to realise it's not the same person. Jackson went to Utah to lay low until he was safe to get out. He knew that Ahmir would stop at nothing to get him killed. Immediately after hiring Michael, he exchanged identities with him. Michael was now Jackson.

Jackson was too smart and had everything planned out. He knew that for him to be able to see his son was up to the law to lift the restraining order. For that to happen it relied on one of two things, and those are for him to die or prove that Ahmir is a wicked tongue twister of an animal. Despite the restraining order he could have just gone to get his son, but he didn't know where they moved to if they had really moved. Even if he knew, he wouldn't just go to get him because Toby wouldn't run with him, they had turned him against his own father.

Jackson already hired Sam, a private investigator, to trace Toby's movements and intended to hire a qualified IT technician whom he came across while surfing the internet so that once Ahmir decide to strike, he would know. The name he found was Muhamad. He called Muhamad and scheduled a meeting for the next day. Muhamad instructed him to put on a grey suit and a red tie.

MEANWHILE IN LOUISIANA…….

Toby was in tears when Naomi found him at their favourite rock. "Toby I've been looking for you, I even went to your home" said Naomi, patting him on the shoulder. He replied in an aggressive tone, "what? they told you that I'm a looser whose father deserted to decompose off like dirt." Naomi was puzzled by Toby's reply towards her, she knew that the Toby she knew would never say something like that. "don't worry babe, I'm here for you, whenever you feel like releasing." she assured him.

She gave him a long tight hug, one that would make you want to not let go. The two began walking home holding hands. They were a few miles away when they realised, they have been followed. They increased their pace thinking that their mysterious follower would also adjust with their pace but the man following them took a turn. They became relaxed again as they assumed it was just a pedestrian stretching his legs.

It was getting late when they paused next to Naomi's home. A fairy-tale land it became when they exchanged thy tongues. The mighty ye flying in the dark bluish sphere. Stars shining so bright that Naomi's eyes became clearer and more beautiful than before, the two mouths marinated each other under a full moon. Toby then accompanied Naomi home before heading to his. "We were so worried sick about you, where have you been?" asked Sarah. He told them where he had been. "A fine lady Naomi is, you should not tear her heart son" Ahmir said to

him in an unconvincing tone. Sarah then told him
to eat then prepare himself for the next day.

CHAPTER 1: BULLET SERVED ON A SILVERPLATTER

The pigeons yawned while the sun revealed itself towards its shift once more, for it was a brand-new day. Toby jumped from his bed and prepared for school while Ahmir was busy preparing for his mission and Sarah preparing breakfast. It was during breakfast when they had someone knocking at the door. "Who is it?" Ahmir asked as the head of the house. The knocker did not respond and so Ahmir asked again but still heard no reply. A cold tingling sensation suddenly rushed through Ahmir's body for he was aware that he has made himself an enemy not only to Jackson but to many others.

He slowly walked towards the window to look at who it was. It was Naomi. Ahmir then told Toby that Naomi was at the door. Toby packed his schoolbag, rushed to the door, immediately said his goodbyes, and rushed to school with Naomi.

(ON THEIR WAY TO SCHOOL.TOBY WAS QUIET AND THIS DIDN'T SIT WELL WITH NAOMI)

Naomi: what's going on munchie?

Toby: Nothing is going on, just that I've been thinking a lot lately

Naomi: Oh! I have a bad feeling about your sudden "thinking a lot" are you maybe reconsidering us, our Relationship?

Toby: Lol no, relax babe, I've been thinking about how my dad deserted me in my final year and how

Ahmir is being acting strange lately.

Naomi: sorry about all that babe but why are u referring your uncle by his name?

Toby: That man, my uncle? Nah, he doesn't deserve it. I swear he is cooking something

Naomi: Boy you've got some anger issues (replied in laughter)

Their conversation was stopped by principal Rogers who told them to rush to their classes before the bell rings.

Few hours later in Utah......

Jackson was on his way to Puro where he was supposed to meet with Muhamad, the IT genius, when his car broke down. He became frustrated till a black Mercedes came to the rescue. "Hey pal! Need a lift?" the man in the car politely asked. "I would appreciate that man." He replied. The man told him that his name was CJ short for Chris Jonathan and Jackson told him his name. CJ told him that he came to Utah to complete a 5minute job so he could collect his pay cheque. Jackson was beginning to ask himself a lot of questions, one of them being the type of job that only requires minutes till he saw a gun in the car.

The car reached its destination and to Jackson's astonishment CJ also got off. Jackson went into the restaurant while CJ went into the opposite building carrying a large violin case, or so it looked like. Thanks to the dress code, Muhamad spotted him very quick and immediately pointed a table for him to sit. They shook hands just like ordinary businesspeople would do, sat down, and started exchanging words.

Jackson told Muhamad about his plan and told him what he was needed for. He then gave him a brown envelope containing pictures of Ahmir, address, and everything he knew about him. Immediately after finalising the contract and Jackson was heading towards the exit, a gunshot was fired from a mile. It aimed for someone else but unfortunately it hit Jackson. He stood there in pain; his chest bleeding heavily that the grey suit darkened with red. The hitman missed his target. By the time the ambulance got there Jackson had already suffered a lot of blood, in a state that required an intensive care unit. They took him to the hospital where he was donated blood and taken care of. On that very same night Michael Burrows got into a car accident just outside Utah and was taken to the nearest hospital, Piero Santino hospital. The same hospital where Jackson was admitted. The two of them had lost a great amount of blood and both were in overly critical conditions as they couldn't breathe independently.

Of course, news travels fast especially to those who keep inserting their noses to peoples' businesses. 24 hours later after Jackson hospitalisation the news had already reached Louisiana; Ahmir. He didn't want Toby to know that his father was shot and hospitalised because he knew the emotions the incident would provoke hence leading to Toby wanting to spend some time with his father. Ahmir didn't think Jackson would make it after hearing that he had lost a lot of blood, but he had to make sure that he really kicks the bucket. He then ordered one of the nurses to switch off the machine before he resurrects. Little did he know, Muhamad had already set off his work and somehow managed to get into his phone remotely, recording and overhearing his conversations while doing so. The next day he, Muhamad, headed to the hospital but just couldn't believe the music he felt hitting his ears. "Sir, are you okay, is the anything else you would like to know?" the doctor enquired with him while tapping him on his left shoulder. he wanted the doctor to explain again what had happened. "Mr, the person you are looking for, Jackson Smith, is no more; we found the machine that was supplying him with oxygen unplugged" the doctor further explained "I promise you the situation is being handled as we speak; as of now the department of health together with independent research and investigation institutions are trying to get to the

centre of the matter as to make sure that the
person behind the murders be put behind bars."

Immediately after hearing this Muhamad stood up
with a smile on his face and went home leaving
the doctor in shock for it was his first time seeing
someone welcome such news with a smile.

CHAPTER 1:
RESURRECTION:
GHOST ON THE MOVE

Ahmir was excited to hear the wonderful news that Sophia had for him, the nurse that pulled the plug. She confirmed with him and even send her a picture of Jackson's dead body. He couldn't wait to finalise everything hence immediately after receiving the news he informed the family elders and arranged for a family meeting scheduled for the following day, the aim was to address everyone.

Meanwhile all hell broke loose at the hospital which Jackson was held in. They were looking for the culprit who swear an oath but later took a life. AS the saying goes, never judge a book by its cover, Sophia was too good for her work hence they couldn't find anything. The next day came, and the meeting went ahead as planned. "I stand in front of you all with a heart that's shattered into pieces as to address the painful news I received yesterday from my friend who's working at Piero Santino Hospital" paused for a moment as to wipe the fake tears, "Jackson is no more, unfortunately he left us. I was hoping we.......

Toby stood up as he cried heading for the door, he just couldn't believe he lost all his parents. Ahmir's wife tried running for him while Ahmir was finishing his statement, "I was hoping we could go to claim his body tomorrow."

The elders agreed with him. By the time Sarah got outside Toby was nowhere to be found. Michael burrows was discharged the next morning from the hospital, Piero Santino Hospital. They told him to call a family member to take him home that's when he took his phone and called Muhamad. On their way home they decided to go to the government mortuary to claim the body, Jackson's body. A few minutes later when Ahmir and the rest of the family got there the body was nowhere to be found. The elders were puzzled and as for Ahmir, he was left a fool. They then travelled back home after being told that the body was claimed a few minutes before they arrived and that the claimers immediately took the body.

Muhamad and Michael were able to locate Jackson's real family using his real name, Michael burrows. After doing so Muhamad with the help of his intelligent brain was able to defeat the state's firewalls thus removing any death file that stated that Jackson was dead and corrected the name to Michael Burrows. All that was left was for the mission to end.

Meanwhile in Louisiana the family couldn't believe the news brought back by Ahmir and the two elders he was with. They started questioning themselves. Toby rushed to the room where everybody was in. "is it true? Is it true that my father is dead?" he asked in a heart-breaking tone, a tone of someone who had lost hope. Sarah went to him and said to whispered to him "you have us son, you will never be alone."

The following day Toby was on his way from school with Naomi after writing their final exam. He was busy telling Naomi about his father's death when a car came at a high speed from behind and braked next to them, he looked like the mysterious follower that followed them the other day. He told him to get in, but he didn't want to. He asked for the second time with a mean face but that made Toby suspicious that's when he took Naomi's hand. "Your father!" he reached out to him with his voice just as they had begun their marathon. They came to a stop. The man approached them with a slow drive and then came to a stop near them. "I have been watching you ever since the day your father told me to do so. Even now I was sent to you by him." He explained to Toby,

"My father is dead, so what are you talking about?" Toby asked him. He was close to lashing out when the mysterious follower replied to him "my name is Sam, a private investigator working for your father and your father is still alive. It is an awfully long and complicated story, but I can call him right now if you want. Sam took out his phone and called Jackson. Immediately after hearing his father's voice on the other side, he took the phone. "Dad is this really you?"

"Yes, it is me, son. Now look I don't want to jeopardise the mission, just know that I'm coming for you son, I'm doing it for you, my only son" Jackson replied

"no one, absolutely no one should know that you spoke to your father. Let it be a secret"

He then gave him a paper with his numbers on it. "Inform me of every move Ahmir takes. just text me." Sam said to him before driving off like a lunatic. They stood there for a while, puzzled, and hungry for answers before continuing their journey to home. Meanwhile Ahmir was trying to come with a plan to get his hands on the inheritance. He stood from where he was sitting and went to the older who were still wondering what had happened. "I got a call from the mortuary, apparently the reason why we did not find his body it's because he was cremated hence, I'm going to get his ashes tomorrow." He then told them to arrange a ceremony to put the remains to rest

The elders were just concerned about burying him and did not hesitate to believe him. When Toby entered the house, Ahmir told him about the call and that he was going to collect the ashes the next day to put his soul to rest. Toby did not want to raise an alarm and so he said to him "at least we will all find the closure; I just want all this to be over." He then went to his room. Later that night Ahmir made a call to Joseph, his old pal. He told him to get him ashes. He then went to collect them the next day and the ceremony went as planned. Later that day the family held a family meeting together with the lawyer in charge of Jackson's assets to discuss the passing of the inheritance to the next kin. The lawyer did not know that Jackson was still alive as he too got confirmation that he was dead. It was 1900 in the evening when the place got filled with sirens, police sirens. Everybody in the house was quite alarmed even the lawyer too. Finally, a sound came through a loudspeaker from outside. "Ahmir Owens, this is detective Joshua from the Louisiana police station, please step outside with your arms over your head."- he loud-spoke.

Ahmir ran towards the backdoor and through it he could see the other cops surrounding the house. The was nowhere to run for he was surrounded. He had no choice but to give in. he slowly walked to the front door where the sound from the loudspeaker came from. The elders were shocked. He opened the door, immediately after stepping outside he was told to get on his knees. Detective Joshua was about to handcuff him when Sarah ran outside fuming, trying to talk his way out but the detective didn't give a care. The detective then said to him "Ahmir Owens, you are under arrest for ordering a hit on, and for the murder of Michael Burrows. You have the right to remain silent, everything you say may and will be used against you in court."

"Who the f**k is Michael Burrows! I don't know who that person is, do you even know who I am, I f**ken own you low-class b****!

"You better watch your tone young man. Everything you say could be used against you in the court of law" said detective Joshua.

She, Sarah, then ran into the house to grab the car keys. She and other two elders drove behind, following the police from the house to the station. When they got there, immediately after parking the car she got out of the car on turbo feet, leaving a gap between her and the two elders who were running as fast as two hungry tortoises. She got in there and ran to detective Joshua hoping to interrogate him. "Care to explain why you disrupted our peace just to drag my husband like a dog?" she asked.

"Mam, with all due respect, the law is the law and consequently, it must be adhered to" he said to her while opening the door to his office.

 "Your husband committed a crime, and by a crime I mean a profoundly serious one. There is evidence that came through and witnesses who are willing to testify. At this case I doubt a bail would be given. So, my advice to you madam is that you get him a great lawyer, a really great lawyer otherwise he is going down, very hard!"- he said, before pointing her to the door. She knew that there was nothing she could do.

Everyone was asleep when she got home. As for Toby he hoped that his father came with the cops that night. Maybe it was too late for him to come, he thought. The next day, early in the morning Sarah took out her phone and called the lawyer. She told him what happened and where her husband, Ahmir, was held. Their lawyer, Jason, went there immediately after the call to see him. "I am here to see Ahmir Owens, please, I am his lawyer"-he said to one of the officers in charge. "I am going to need to see your ID and your work document"- the officer responded to him. immediately after being showed the documents, he called one of the guards on duty to go summon him. "Ahmir Owens, you've got a visitor"-the guard said to him.

He stood up from his bunk and headed to the visitation room. He could not properly walk, and his face was decorated with bruises. "You have to get me out of here otherwise I will come out as a corpse" he said to his lawyer. "What happened to you, you do not even have 24 hours inside these walls, but you are already a target?" Jason said to him

"What can I say mate? I always had a lot of enemies." Ahmir replied. Ahmir and Jason have been friends ever since their primary schooling days hence it was easy for either one of them to say anything they want without the other one feeling offended. Ahmir then began narrating his story, of how he became decorated with bruises. He then said to him "do all you can to get me out of here and oh, before it slips my mind, I need some cash right now to buy myself some protection and some drugs too, maybe cigarettes."

"don't worry my friend, you are going to get bail. I am going to make sure of that and if they deny you bail, I will then make sure that we go to court early so that we can get this thing over and done with" Jason assured him. He then gave me him some few dollars so that he could get himself some protection in the inside. Immediately after they parted Jason tried all he could to get him bail but it was denied. Ahmir was carried back to his cell, awaiting trial which was scheduled to take place a week from then. During that time, he was busy planning how he would escape from prison or in case he gets transferred to another prison. That was not the only tricks he, Ahmir, had. He called one of his goons to visit him immediately after he was granted his call. As for Toby, well, he couldn't wait for the whole thing to end so that he could reunite with his father.

It was a while later when Ahmir was taken out of his cell to the visitation room, his people were there, the goons he ordered to visit him, his servants. They were five in number, pretending as if they were from a local government association called HTWC (Helping the Wrongfully Convicted)

AHMIR: I call one and you come as a community! Well, anyway, I need you to do something for me, a loose end that's preventing us from tasting the bigger cake, real moolah baby! (He said to them, also using hand gestures)

GOON 1: we're all ears boss

AHMIR: His name is Jackson. Jackson Smith. I need you to track him down, till and till you find him. If you don't find him with that name, try Michael Burrows. I believe you know what to do with him. Free him away from my world. OH, before I forget refrigerating his head, I will need to see it. You know, serve it to his boy after sucking them dry. It is the beginning of the end of the Smith's empire, but before you do that, get his boy for me; I will need him as insurance. That's not the only thing I have for you, I need you to organize transport and more power just so it happens that I get transferred to another prison after my trial which is scheduled to take place a few weeks from now.

GOONS: We got you man (all responding at the same time)

Immediately after getting done with Ahmir, they conducted their received instructions and began looking for Jackson.

Meanwhile….

The house was silent when they heard the doorbell ring. "Toby check who's at the door!" Sarah's voice echoed all the way from upstairs. She thought it was the lawyer she was waiting for.

"it's probably the neighbours, I just don't understand why people can be so noisy"- one of the elderlies exclaimed. "Toby!" she shouted, "where the hell is this boy."

"I sent him to make an errand for me," one of the elders said. The doorbell rang once more. "Coming!" she shouted once more. She rang to the door. What she found there was not something she expected. "Jackson" she said disappointedly, "what are you doing here after all that you have done?"

"Is that a great way to welcome your own blood?" Jackson asked," I have to say, it is fun being the one who laughs last. I mean, after all the things your husband has done to me, my son, for heaven's sake, you were like a little sister to my late wife, and to be honest with you, the only reason I agreed to let Toby live with you was because of you, your presence.", he paused for a moment. Sarah could not bear looking at him, all she did was look down, ashamed of herself and what she had become. "Or do I need to remind you that you used to be friends with her? All that running around, sharing secrets, and going places you used to do when you were kids. I'm disappointed in you!

Sarah's phone rang, saving her from the intense moment she found herself in before Jackson. It was a private number, but she answered it anyway.

"Hello," she answered the phone.

"Sarah," Ahmir replied.

"Ahmir! How and where did you get a mobile phone?" she asked.

"That does not matter, what matters is what I'm about to tell you, I need you to do something for me"-Ahmir.

"Okay, I'm all ears."

"My people are on their way to take Toby away as we speak, I need you to corporate so that those things don't escalate out of hand. They will get there before Jackson does." Ahmir replied.

Sarah: what do you mean by your people?

Ahmir: just do as I say, okay!

She immediately noticed that one plus one wasn't two. She looked at Jackson for a few seconds before giving out a reply to Ahmir. Jackson's words might have penetrated through to her brain. She finally said to him, "that's a little too late, Jackson is already here."

Immediately after hearing this, Ahmir dropped the call, he got pissed. Meanwhile Jackson was shocked by Sarah's sudden change of mind. "Take Toby and go!" she said to Jackson. She then told her Ahmir's plan, and how he was planning to abduct Toby.

"Where the hell is he?" he asked. "Toby!" he shouted, repeatedly. "The elders sent him to the shop, he should be back from now," Sarah said.

Jackson looked at his watch, calculating the amount of time it would take Ahmir's men to reach the house.

"Dad!" he said hesitantly. He couldn't believe his eyes.

"Son!" Jackson shouted out of excitement before running to hug him. "Go get your most valuable things, we must go. NOW!"

Toby ran into the house without asking questions. He quickly packed his possessions. Running downstairs, he nearly collided into one of the elders. "Where are the painkillers, I sent you to buy, and why are you in such a hurry?" the elder asked.

"Sorry grandma, I nearly forget, here are the painkillers. My dad is here to pick me up, Bye!" he replied. When Ahmir's men got there, they were nowhere to be found.

They ran to the car, vanishing into time without looking back. "that's a cute bracelet by the way, where did you get it" Jackson complimented Toby's bracelet. "My girlfriend got it for me, she is also wearing one of the same kinds as we speak. We made a vow to each other, that no matter what barrier lies between us, whether distance or time, our love will always find a way to bring us together. The bracelet serves as a reminder of all that we've been through.," he replied. This left Jackson speechless for a while.

"You do know that you will have to notify her, right?"

"Is that a rhetorical question?" he said, before the two busted into laughter.

"I wish I was there to watch you as you transitioned into the young man you are today," he said.

"You are here now, that's all that matters," he replied.

Chapter IIII: f-word the law

23/10/2019, San Francisco high court

The utterances of people elevated as time went by. People were growing more impatient as seconds accumulated into minutes. In the crowds were Muhamad and CJ. From the numbers, one would swear they were awaiting a being of great honour. Things got even worse when Ahmir was brought before the house.

Officer: All rise in court!

They stood up as the law-passer walked into the house of law.

She stood firm and imperious, even the bravest in the room wouldn't dare look into her eyes.

She said to advance the hearing, "this court is now in session. The people will be seated"

Everyone sat as she stared at the papers in front of her, she held them as though they had wronged her. She then looked down to where the accused was seated.

Judge: may the accused be brought forward!

Ahmir hesitates for a while, but the look he received from the judge forced him to stand.

The noise escalated to cloud mode. With every being in the house craving to get their fair pieces of him. The elders, in their hearts were hope, for they didn't know the whole story. They thought he was wrongfully accused and that, Jackson was just a sore loser, who lost her wife, abandoned his son, and later wanted to make Sarah witness the pain he went through when he lost his beauty of a wife. the process went on and on till time to call on the first witness arrived.

"Order in court!" she roared from her sit, leaving the house shaken by fear. The house came to an abrupt silence before she could proceed with the process.

Judge: MR. Ahmir Owens, you stand accused of multiple crimes including the embezzlement of funds, murder of Michael Burrows, and attempted murder of Jackson Smith. How do you plead?

Ahmir: not guilty your honour!

Judge: very well, then. Mr Owens, you may approach the stand.

Ahmir walked to the box beside the judge's desk.

Judge: will the prosecution please rise?

The lawyer rose from where he was seated. Tall brown, eye-seducing pupils, a nice blend of white and melanin, fancy suit, and a diamond watch welded to his left arm. He cleared his throat before commencing with his prosecution.

Prosecutor: Mr. Owens, did you murder Michael burrows, steal the funds Jackson sent to you for his son, and attempt to kill Jackson Smith?

Ahmir: of course not. I didn't do all those things.

Ahmir was calm throughout the whole thing for he knew that no matter the verdict the result would be him roaming free out of prison.

Prosecutor: you didn't pay someone else to commit these crimes for you?

Ahmir: I did not.

Prosecutor: what's your relationship with Jackson Smith?

Ahmir: he was married to my sister, Gladys, the mother to Toby.

Prosecutor: have you ever heard of the name 'Sophia'?

Ahmir: I have met thousands of people with that name.

Prosecutor: well then, let me be specific. Do you know anyone by that name working at Piero Santino hospital.

Ahmir: Yes, she was my primary school friend.

Prosecutor: let's go back to night of 22 September 2018. Where were you on that night Mr Owens?

Ahmir: I was at home.

Prosecutor: did you or did you not get in contact with your "primary school friend", Sophia?

Ahmir: I did.

Prosecutor: let me get this right. on the night of 22 September 2018, the same night Jackson smith was shot and hospitalized, you decided to check on your primary school friend. Sounds to me like you ordered a hit on Mr Smith, just so to finish him while he is we….

"Objection your honour!"

Jason spoke up while everyone was asleep.

Judge: objection sustained Mr Kruger.

Jason: your honour the prosecutor is playing mind games on my client further passing over judgement without proof. Besides that, the responsibility of reaching a verdict is not up to him.

Judge: Mr Thon, please refrain from doing such!

Prosecutor: I'm sorry your honour.

Prosecutor: when is the last time you talked to Sophia Mr Owens?

Ahmir: on that very same night. The night of the 22nd of September 2018.

Prosecutor: correct me if I'm wrong Mr Ahmir Owens. So, you and Sophia are not that close friends, and you don't talk that often?

Ahmir: even close friends do not need to talk every day. What kind of a stupid question is that?

Judge: Mr Owens, please refrain from using such language in the court of law. This is my house, and you shall adhere to my rules. Please answer the question laid to your response.

Ahmir: we are close friends.

Prosecutor: well, then, when was the last time you saw her?

Ahmir: 3years back.

Prosecutor: that doesn't sound like being close friends Mr Owens.

Ahmir: well than I guess everyone has their own definition of close friends.

Prosecutor: what is your definition of a close friend Mr Owens?

Jason stepped in again

Jason: Objection! Your honour Mr Thon is asking questions not related to the case beforehand.

Judge: objection sustained. Mr Thon could you please ask questions only related to the case?

Prosecutor: okay your honour.

Meanwhile in Finberg, 30minutes away from San Francisco …

"don't go anywhere until I'm back Toby" Jackson said to his son.

Toby: But dad I told you I had to see Naomi today.

Jackson: No buts, Toby. Just do as I say!

The house was guarded by five well trained security guards. Jackson knew exactly what Ahmir was capable of and didn't want to risk taking chances.

Back in San Francisco….

(The court advanced)

Prosecutor: Ms Sophia Gruevski, do you swear an oath that you will tell nothing but only the truth?

Sophia: I Sophia Gruevski swear an oath that I will tell nothing but only the truth.

Prosecutor: should you be found to violate the purpose of the oath, lying to the house at large, there are and will be consequences to be suffered.

Prosecutor: okay now, Ms Gruevski, do you know Mr Ahmir Owens?

Sophia: yes, I do Sir.

Prosecutor: what's your relationship with Mr Owens mam?

Sophia: we used to attend primary school together.

Prosecutor: would you say you two are close friends?

Sophia: No sir.

Prosecutor: please elaborate.

Sophia: we met last year in January at an event organised by WHO for the first time in 16years. I was going through a rough time, with no money to pay for my kids' education. He then offered to pay for them also giving me $50000 in cash to pay off my rent.

Prosecutor: so, in other words you felt like you were obliged to him?

Sophia: yes sir.

Prosecutor: Did Mr Owens get in contact with you after that day and if so, when?

Sophia: yes, he did, I think the date was the 22nd of September 2018.

Prosecutor: You think?

Sophia: it was on the 22nd of September 2018 sir!

Prosecutor: did he tell you to do anything out of law for him Ms Gruevski?

(Sophia takes a while, looking at Ahmir before the prosecutor repeated the question.)

Prosecutor: Ms Gruevski! Did he task you to anything that is out of law for him?

Sophia: yes, he did.

Prosecutor: and what was that?

Sophia: he asked me to finish a man by the name of Jackson Smith.

Prosecutor: finish? That's a little harsh Ms Gruevski. So those were his words?

Sophia: yes Sir.

Prosecutor: that is all I have for now your honour.

Judge: you can take your seat now Mr Thon.

Jason stood up from his sitting, prepared to defend his client and friend.

Jason: Ms Gruevski: do you have proof that my client called you on the 22nd of September 2018?

Sophia: no sir. My old phone got lost, in it was my call history.

Jason: you honour I don't have anything more to say, as the saying goes "innocent until proven guilty.

An officer ran to the judge with a tape.

Officer: your honour, someone just dropped this off, he didn't leave a name. but he said it's evidence, proof that Ahmir ordered Sophia to kill Jackson.

Judge: new evidence just came in, a tape containing evidence of Ahmir Owens Calling Sophia Gruevski as so to put a bounty on Jackson's head.

The house at large was shocked, even Ahmir himself.

The judge ordered them to play the tape, in it was a conversation which conspired between Ahmir and Sophia. The elders were shocked to find out that their favourite Son was a monster, not Jackson.

Jason: for all we know that tape could have been produced with the help of modern technology!

Judge: Mr Owens is that you?

Ahmir: NO! I'm not evil your honour.

Judge: Mr Gruevski, you can now take your seat, your matter will be sent out to the relevant authorities.

After a while, the next witness was called to stand, Jackson himself. He walked into the house, Ahmir, for someone who was about to experience what life imprisonment was, eventually leading to the chair, was happy to see him. before the judge was about to give command for the court to proceed, Jason stood up in a haste, asking the judge for permission to answer a call. When the judge looked at him and asked for the level of significance of the call, he sweetened what was not the truth even worse. "My wife is in a Coma; she has been for the past 6 months." He paused to inhale, "a call from the hospital, I don't want to lose her"

The whole court went soft on him, "aww," they all said. The judge, out of sympathy gave him permission to take the call. After a while of being outside, he came in, with a big smile on his face.

Judge: good news, I guess?

Jason: my wife made it out of the coma.

The house at large went crazy, everyone was passing out congratulations at him. little did they know he was on a mission; he nodded his head for Ahmir to see. That's when he confidently, stood up from his sitting, ruining the celebration.

Ahmir: okay, okay! People, this was a waste of my time. You know what! all of you are a waste of my time!

The court: Ah! (Shocked by the rude behaviour portrayed by Ahmir)

Judge: Mr Owens could you please take your seat.

Ahmir: don't tell me what to do, look, you look ridiculous. I ordered a hit in Jackson, stole the money, guilty is my middle name!

The court: Ah! (Once again, the court, screamed out of shock)

Judge: are you saying that you are guilty of all the charges mentioned at the commencing of the court Mr Owens?

Ahmir: yes, I am, I am proud that I did it. The world needs more people like me, action takers not people who plan but don't execute.

The elders: what!

Together with most of the people vouching for him, they were all shocked to their greatest imagination.

Judge: are you sure Mr Owens?

Ahmir: I'm very sure your honour.

Judge: the court, passing down of the sentence will resume after 15 minutes. I must discuss with the panel to discuss a more suitable sentence for you.

The judge discussed with the panel to suggest a way forward. They talked till it seemed like they came to an agreement.

Judge: Mr Owens, the court finds you guilty in all charges laid against you, hence sentencing you to 50years at fox river without parole.

The judge called for him to be taken to his holding cell where he would be temporarily held caged like the animal he is. All those, in support of him were disappointed, Jackson, Jackson was happy to witness his biggest hater being dragged forcefully out of the court.

The family, one by one went to bid farewell to Ahmir, of course the words coming out of the elders' mouths were unkind, some even cursed the day he was brought into this world. Sarah's mouth remained shut as the elders retaliated with words. He had never seen his wife like that, troubled and mad, she looked.

Ahmir: can I please speak to my wife please? Alone!

The elders left the two in a haste.

Ahmir: hey, are you okay?

Sarah: okay? You took it too far Ahmir! So, all this time I was dating a murderer, I shared blankets with you knowing very well you have blood on your hands. I hope you rot in hell Ahmir; I really do!

Sarah! Sarah!

Okay fine then, I don't need you, you hear me, I don't need you. I see you forget we were in this together…. you are just a selfish daughter of a bustard!" Anger, up and down his veins, it walked tall. "You will regret your words; I'll be out of here sooner than you think. Mark my words."

Sarah could still hear his voice echoing through the walls. He kept on shouting till she saw the outside of the court walls.

.

F-word the law;, let there be carnage!

Guard: Owens, your transport is waiting for you outside. Please turn against the wall with your arms above your head!

Owens: hahahaha! You are all fools, everything, the law, people, you all are fools, nincompoops!

Guard: at least we are not the ones locked up in a prison. We are fools who live by the law.

Ahmir: which law, the constitution which was created by man so as to hide all the dirty things they do behind your back. See brother let me ask you a question, how many African people get shot each day by the very same police who are supposed to protect us?

The guard didn't say a word. Of course, the answer to Ahmir's question was an obvious one.

Ahmir: exactly, a lot. I'll just shut my mouth, laugh at all of you as you are being made fools by your own governments.

Guard: just do that for me my friend.

Just like that, our favourite villain Ahmir was on his way to a maximum jail, or so they thought.

The truck was heavily secured with two other cars accompanying it. Little did they know what he had up his sleeves. The trucks were loaded with webcams which would upload its feed every 4hours.

Ahmir's is a master-manipulator. He knows how to use words to get whatever it is that he wants. The guard, who took him out of his cell had told Ahmir's men the road that they were going to take. The cams started jamming and everything going off, chaos is what was about to go down. The guards thought it was just a temporary thing, till one of the cars accompanying Ahmir got blown up on the spot. The cars came to an abrupt stop, with Ahmir laughing out loud.

"what's wrong with you, you think this is a joke!?," one of the guards, fuming with anger asked.

"what's wrong with me?" he laughed," I'll tell you what is wrong with me, the fact that you are all fools, hahahaha!"

It wasn't long till the guards in the second vehicle were taken out cold blooded on the spot. Just like that, he had won again.

"Who and what the hell is this?" Ahmir asked, just before he sat down.

"Your get-out-of-prison gift boss," one of Ahmir's men said.

Chapter II: TEMPORARY ALLIANCE

"Officer, I need to file in a missing person case, my son, my son...."

Officer: sir, please calm down, and explain what is going on.

Jackson: my son went missing and the whole house is a mess, I believe Ahmir had something to do with it.

Officer: that's quite an accusation sir, you know you could be arrested for defamation of character, right?

Jackson: I don't care about all that, are you going to help me or what?

officer: relax sir, I am going to help you right now. You said something about Ahmir having something to with it, how is that possible because he mis on his way to prison right now? Maybe your son decided to throw a little party on his way out.

Jackson: then how do you explain the six security guards who I found dead in my yard?

The officer stood there, shocked for a while before proceeding to reply.

Officer: come with me. Detective, detective!

 He raised his voice once more.

This is Jackson Smith, Jackson this is detective Grobler. Jackson here has one interesting case, the kind you love solve. "Believe me Jason, me and my friend here are well acquainted, we used to be childhood besties."

 Jackson was in the middle of his conversation with Grobler when a lady officer walked in.

Lady officer: sir, you have to see this!

Detective: see what?

Lady officer: turn on the TV right now.

Ahmir's escape had made headlines. Jackson immediately flew from his seat, leaving his sit, with the detective following to stop him. you could just see from the look on his face that something terrible and horrifying was about to go down.

Detective Grobler: hey! Jackson! Jackson! where are you going?

Jackson didn't bother looking back, all he had to say was that he was going to fetch his son.

Detective Grobler: think before you act, okay fine let's say he has your son, don't you think this whole thing is a trap?

Jackson, fuming out with anger, sweat pouring from his face, and his face painted with muscular veins; "what do you expect I do huh!? Sit back while that animal kills my son? I don't think so!

Detective Grobler: I shall assemble a team composed of only the best on this matter. I swear we will find your son.

Jackson stopped for a few seconds, turned his face to look at detective Grobler one more time as though he was considering his proposal, "we'll see who gets there first!" then stormed out of the police station. The detective was left shocked, for he was speechless, wondering what was running through his mind. The first thing he, Jackson, did, when he stepped into the car, was to make a phone call.

"Call the team, 987 southwest, pilchards hotel, room45!"

Meanwhile in Turuu, town found in the middle of Louisiana, a remote area, characterized of poor structures:

"We will end this now and for all, we have come far, read through pages of this war. My friends you have grown in front of my eyes, became the men you are, fearless, strong, dangerous, and above all, powerful." He said before pausing to take a drink.

"We are who we believe we are, and money is what keeps us all alive, TO POWER!"

"TO POWER!" they all yelled.

MY SON, MY EVERYTHING

He went ahead, removing the sack on Toby's face, "I want you to watch as I spill your father's blood, the floor will be red, the sky will turn clear blue, my bank account will be fattened, all will be well. But first, my friend over here will do us the honours." He then looked at all the men in the room before bringing an end to his speech,

"let's begin!"

987 SOUTHWEST, PILCHARDS HOTEL, ROOM45

"Don't worry we will find Ahmir," said Muhamad

"I don't care about Ahmir, all I want is MY SON, he is MY EVERYTHING!"

"What do you intend to do when you get there?" asked Muhamad. "Only God knows."

Just as Muhamad was searching through the dark web and all sorts of hidden corners of the internet, his screen suddenly went black before resurfacing with a live video.

 The first thing that hit Jackson was Toby screaming for help, crying as he was being tortured by Ahmar's men. Dressed in a red cable and a mask covering the whole of his face, holding a whip on Toby's neck.

"Jackson, oh Jackson! If you still want your precious son, you know what to do, transfer

10million dollars to the account number on the bottom of the screen. I believe you are wise enough to know when to quit. I saw your little quarrel with Ahmar, I know you can afford it. 24hours, that's all you have, 24 hours!"

The screen went blank again and eventually shutting down.

"Did you get it, the location?" asked Jackson.

"They are just a couple of rookies; they know nothing about technology. They are in Turuu, 454 Lilian Street, but who on earth is the red cable guy?" He spoke.

"it's probably a decoy Ahmir is using to fool me into transferring money into his account" so, replied to Jackson.

Just as the two were exchanging words, the phone rang, it was Sam.

"CJ and I just came back from digging around. Ahmar is working with the most unreliable yet dangerous man on earth. His name is Sohomoskialatto Gongruo Mario, also known as the red cableman. He is wanted in over 30 countries worldwide for homicides and human trafficking. Chances are he is going to kill both Ahmir and Toby one he asks his account is blessed. He usually asks for ransoms and kills once he gets it. We are on our way there"

"We are heading to Turuu, we'll meet you just outside the border," said Muhamad.

Meanwhile in Turuu:

"Hey, you! what are you gossiping about?" angry Ahmar asked.

The red cableman winked at the guy behind Ahmar.

"What's that, what are you doing? I own the whole operation don't forget that!" said Ahmar.

"That my friend is Malkovia" said the red cableman.

"What am I supposed to do with that?" asked Ahmar, as he got more pissed.

"Why don't you turn around and see for yourself."' Said the red cableman.

Ahmir turned around, and what he saw was not impressing at all, all guns were pointing at him. He shook with fear, asking why they had turned on him.

"We know you got cash. See, all this is a meticulously designed plan. It all began when you needed men to conduct all your dirty work at the beginning. I knew it would all come to this. It was a pleasure doing business with you Ahmir. Tie him up"

Ahmir received the punches till he got drunk and surrendered, gave them the money they wanted. He sat there, tied, feeling as though the entire world had turned against him, as if he was finally burning for his sins. Bruised, blood leaking from all over his skin, his face barely unrecognisable due to the blood covering it. They took turns beating him till he spit it all. It was at that moment he knew what he had done was pure evil and way too far from what he initially planned. Ahmir looked back, introspected, and realised what he had lost, a wife, family, relatives, he then knew there was nothing to do but to apologize and go serve his time, which was probably going to be life imprisonment.

Just as Jackson and his crew were on their way, they received a call from the red-cable man. The call was to remind them to wire the money quick otherwise it would be the end of Toby. It was untraceable. Following them was a black Mercedes, dimmed glass, a Turuu number plate. They all couldn't see it. They pulled over a few metres away from the warehouse while the black Mercedes pulled over a few blocks from them, hidden by the trees. Jackson, CJ, and Sam all went in hot. Sam, thanks to his training while at the academy and background in the police force; CJ, thanks to his private training and assassin training; and Jackson, he took some shooting lessons a while ago, you never know how rich people choose to spend their money. They went in hot. He immediately rushed to strangle him. "Where is my son, where the hell is my son Ahmir?" while landing a few punches in between. He gasped for air before he would atter a word.

"Gongrou has him, he said he knew you were dumb enough to try to get him. There is a camera right there." He said, while swallowing his own blood.

"Where in hell's corners did he go!" angry Jackson asked.

"don't kill him man, he might as well be the only person who knows where to find him," said CJ.

"I don't know, okay. I really don't. listen, I'm really sorry man, for everything I've done to you. I'm going to help you find your son. Said Ahmir.

"Why would I trust you, after everything you done, you want me to trust you?" said Jackson.

"I have nothing to lose or gain, so please. I know I can't make up for everything I did, but I will try." Said Ahmir,

They untied him and went with him to the car. "I know of a guy, his name is Solomon, he is the one who helped me find Gongruo. I suggest we go to him, although he'll want a lot of money to tell us the truth." Said Ahmir. "I can give up everything I have just to be with my son again. If I must pay millions, so be it." Said Jackson, before he took out a case underneath the seat. "You caused for all these, and consequently you'll have to pay for all that you have done!"

"So, do you always have money in your car?" said Ahmir before he was met with harsh words coming straight from the whole team. The black Mercedes with dim windows pursued them, slowly, and slowly, seeing everything they did in between, the stops they made, all of them. None of them noticed.

18:47, Turuu Airport, Jackson's jet.

Muhmad: damn! Time flies, what time do you think we'll arrive?

Jackson: according to my research it will take us approximately 8hours to get to malkovia. We'll have enough time to rest in between our current point and the point of destination.

CJ: so, Muhamad, have you already scanned the perimeter?

Muhamad: yeah, its surrounded by bushes, near the Malkovian border.

Ahmir: you all know we going to need guns right, kill everyone!

Jackson: we know what we are doing, and nobody asked for your opinion.

Ahmir: oh, but it is a fact!

CJ: I swear I'll be the first one to put a bullet in between your skull if you don't shut up.

Jackson: just so you know, we are sorted already. See that large black case over there, its equipped with most dangerous weapons known to man.

Little did they know they were being followed by a mystery man.

Jackson kept his guard up, for in case Ahmir tries pulling some tricks up his sleeve. They tied him on the seat as they were about to take a nap. After hours off travelling the finally reached their destination. They immediately got into one of the cars Jackson rented from a car rent company.

And there they went, driving as if they had second lives. Muhamad suddenly broke the silence in the car, "according to Ahmir's guy, they shouldn't be that far."

"Try searching for goldb3425", said Ahmir.

"What's that?" asked Muhamad.

"Oh, it's a tracker," Ahmir replied.

"a tracker?" went everyone at once.

"What? You think I was going to let my meal ticket jut to wander off like that? I did it for in case he tried escaping," said Ahmir.

"Hey! Don't call my son your meal ticket! Don't tell me you put a chip under my son's skin!" said Jackson.

"Sorry man, but I had to find my way under his skin," said Ahmir, continuing to laugh, "You know what I mean?"

"You son of a b****!" the whole gang jumped in to stop Jackson from killing Ahmir. "I'm going to kill you once this whole thing is over!"

"Oh, I found him, they are heading for an abandoned toy factory, called FKJ, 30minutes drive from here." Said Muhamad.

They began loading their guns and going through their plan once more. Minutes, after minutes, there they were going through the details, and getting armed for the great mission. Ahmir was to stay in the car with Muhamad, tied still; Jackson was to walk in with Muhamad, carrying a suitcase with millions in it; whilst CJ was to be stationed a few meters away for sniper shots, Sam was to hide in the trees, near the factory, for closer shots.

03:18am, FKJ:

They arrived at the factory. The other crew members got out of the car, a short distance away from the factory leaving Jackson and Muhamad the only ones in the car. Jackson, carrying a suitcase in his hand, got out of the car at the gate, while Muhamad pretended to drive off.

Jackson: I come with peace. (He yelled at the door)

No one responded, and so he decided to walk into the factory, in it finding Toby tired onto a chair, he ran towards him, yelling out his name. the lights suddenly went lit and they came out, holding guns, distinct kinds of guns. He came to an abrupt stop before talking, gasping for air.

Jackson: I come with peace! Just take the money and give me my son, please!

The red-cable man: yeah, I could have done that, but you chose to follow me her, worst part you come alone, what did you think, huh?

Jackson: please! I'm begging you, just let my son GO!

The red-cable man: untie the boy's mouth, I wat his to scream his father's name, knowing there's nothing he can do about it. Hold our friends head onto the table, I want to cut it off!

(After, he cracked an evil laughter.)

Jackson: no, please, no! (He was frightened)

One of his right-hand men, raised his axle to the air, to cut his head off. Toby screaming out loud, yelling pain out of his mouth.

 The glass, shattered, a shot to the right-hand man's brain. He fell dead, which was before Jackson ran to untie Toby, and the Malkovian gang began falling one by one. CJ kept them coming in hot, before Sam went in on fire. Shots being fired from all angles.

Ahmir was growing impatient in the car.

Ahmir: untie me!

Muhamad: you know I can't do that

Ahmir: we both know that they are outnumbered!

Muhamad, while untying him," try running away and we will hunt you down."

It was all chaos in the building, Ahmir got in there and immediately started killing his fair shots. Blood everywhere, dust, bullets, definitely a confined world war1. Jackson was about to exit the building, carrying Toby, when a bullet went straight for his right leg. He tried pushing but he couldn't get too far. The re-cable man got to him. everything suddenly went quiet; Muhamad couldn't hear anything from where he was. He was terrified and growing impatient.

"You travel miles to kill my men, and you think you'd walk out of it alive? You all are just a bunch of crazies." He paused for his iconic evil laughter, "I have my gun on your leader's head. Guess it's time to say goodbye, huh?"

"Oh, poor Ahmir, lying cold on the floor, you should have just stayed home with your pretty little wife!" said the red-cable man.

"This is FBI, please get out with your hands on top of your head!" suddenly came to their ears. The red-cable men walked out with his gun on Jackson's head while the rest of the team led the way.

"Put your guns down, or I'm blowing his brains out!" said the red-cableman.

Jackson was terrified. As for toby, the tears couldn't dry out. just as the red-cable men was yelling "put them down" repeatedly, a shot landed on his head from the bushes. Both the police and the team were shocked.

"Detective Grobler, TURUU police force," he said, while waving his badge down. "This group of men are a part of a highly secretive mission to put an end to the red-cableman by all means necessary!"

The medic rushed to their assistance. Detective Grobler went to Jackson.

Jackson: how did you know we were here?

Grobler: well, the Jackson I know never backs down, I knew you were going for him. I've being following you ever since that day and you all couldn't notice.

 He paused to laugh. "You better watch over your back my friend, you never know who's following you"

They both laughed.

"Hey!" one of the officers shouted." There's someone coughing in there!"

Just when they were about to rush to save the individual, the places went up all in flames and exploded at once. Toby, in the ambulance, looked at his dad. "Is it over?"

"I hope so. All that matters is that I got you back, son. I love you so much, you are what makes me 'ME,' you are my everything!" said Jackson to his son.

A week later....

Jackson, Sarah, the elders, they hosted a celebration for the return of their beloved Toby. The music, the food, the smiles, everyone was in a good mood. Jackson was happy to see the smiles on Toby's face as he catches up with his girlfriend, Naomi. A courier guy arrived, throwing mail into the yard. One specifically sent to Toby Smith.

Jackson called Toby to inform him about the mail. He ran to open it. Shaken, and frightened, the letter simply slipped from his hands to the ground on knees he went. Jackson, heartbroken by the look on Toby's face, he picked up the letter.

It read "MONEY AND BONDS, for all that matters. Till we meet again. YOUR GREATEST FEAR, XOXO!"

The end is simply the beginning of something greater!